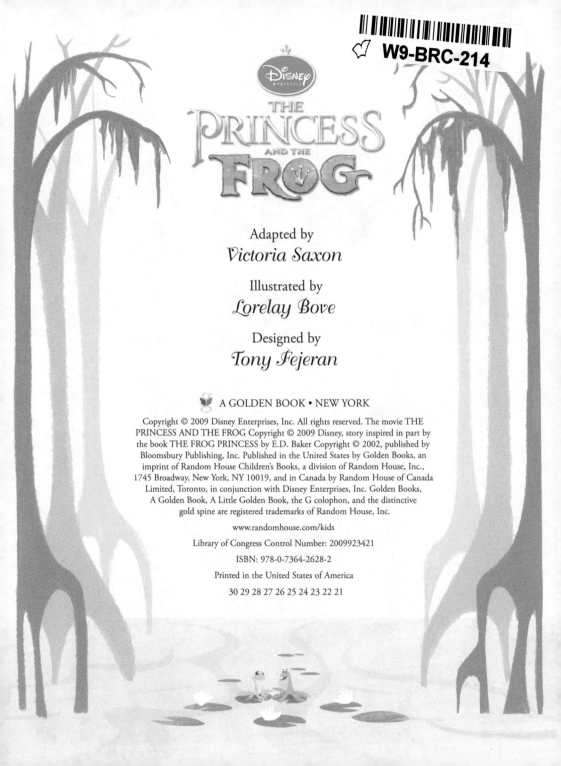

DISNEY
PRINCESS

THE PRINCESS AND THE FROG

Adapted by
Victoria Saxon

Illustrated by
Lorelay Bove

Designed by
Tony Fejeran

A GOLDEN BOOK • NEW YORK

Copyright © 2009 Disney Enterprises, Inc. All rights reserved. The movie THE
PRINCESS AND THE FROG Copyright © 2009 Disney, story inspired in part by
the book THE FROG PRINCESS by E.D. Baker Copyright © 2002, published by
Bloomsbury Publishing, Inc. Published in the United States by Golden Books, an
imprint of Random House Children's Books, a division of Random House, Inc.,
1745 Broadway, New York, NY 10019, and in Canada by Random House of Canada
Limited, Toronto, in conjunction with Disney Enterprises, Inc. Golden Books,
A Golden Book, A Little Golden Book, the G colophon, and the distinctive
gold spine are registered trademarks of Random House, Inc.

www.randomhouse.com/kids

Library of Congress Control Number: 2009923421

ISBN: 978-0-7364-2628-2

Printed in the United States of America

30 29 28 27 26 25 24 23 22 21

When Tiana was a *little* girl, she loved to cook.

"Food brings people together," Tiana's **daddy** always said.

Tiana had a **BIG** dream.
She wanted to own a restaurant
one day. It would have music and
good food—and it would bring
people together, just as Daddy said.

Tiana grew up
and worked
hard.

When she had
saved enough money,
she tried to buy a place
for her own
restaurant.

The two brokers
promised to
sell her the
old sugar
mill.

FENNER
BROS.
REALTY
FOR SALE
SOLD

Tiana went to her friend Charlotte's costume party. There the brokers **broke** their promise.

Tiana was so upset that she **fell** and **ruined** her costume. Her dreams of opening a restaurant were gone.

Charlotte gave Tiana
a pretty princess
costume.

But Tiana
was still
sad.

She saw the **Evening Star** in the sky—and made a wish for her restaurant!

But instead of her restaurant, a frog appeared . . .

. . . and **spoke** to her!

The frog said he was really
a prince named Naveen. A
bad magic man had changed
him into a frog.

Would Tiana kiss him if he
gave her the restaurant?
NO!

Well . . . maybe one
tiny kiss. . . .
SMOOCH!

The frog did not turn into a prince.
But Tiana **TURNED INTO A FROG!**

The frogs fell
off the balcony.

They **bounced**
on some drums.

They *flew* away.

The two frogs ended
up in the bayou. It was
scary there!

A big **bird**
wanted to
eat them.

Alligators
wanted to eat them.

EVERYTHING wanted to eat them!

Tiana and Naveen **escaped!**

Tiana **worked** while
Naveen **played.**

Soon they met an alligator named Louis. Louis loved **jazz**—just like Naveen.

Louis and Naveen **jammed** while Tiana planned.

Soon the frogs were **HUNGRY**. They **tangled** their tongues trying to catch a fly.

A firefly **untangled** them. His name was . . .

Ray and his family **lit** a path through the bayou. The path led to . . .

... Mama Odie!
She told the
frogs to find out
what they needed,
not just what
they wanted.

Then **Mama Odie** told Naveen he had to kiss Tiana's friend Charlotte, who was Mardi Gras princess for the night. Kissing a princess would make both frogs human again!

But the **bad magic** man tried to stop Naveen.

Uh-oh!
The *chase* was on!
Would the frog
kiss the princess
in time?

NO! Time was up. Naveen and Tiana **remained** frogs.

But they realized that they were in **love**. That was all they really **needed**.

The two frogs got married.
Now Tiana was a princess!
That meant that Naveen
finally kissed a princess.

The magic
worked! Both
frogs became
human again!

Tiana and Naveen *worked* hard **TOGETHER** to fix up her restaurant.

It was the **BEST** restaurant ever! At last, Tiana had exactly what she wanted . . .

. . . and exactly what she **needed**—good food and good times with family and friends.